Magic Ballerina ™

Delphie and the Birthday Show

Darcey Bussell

HarperCollins *Children's Books*

*To Phoebe and Zoe, as they are the inspiration
behind Magic Ballerina.*

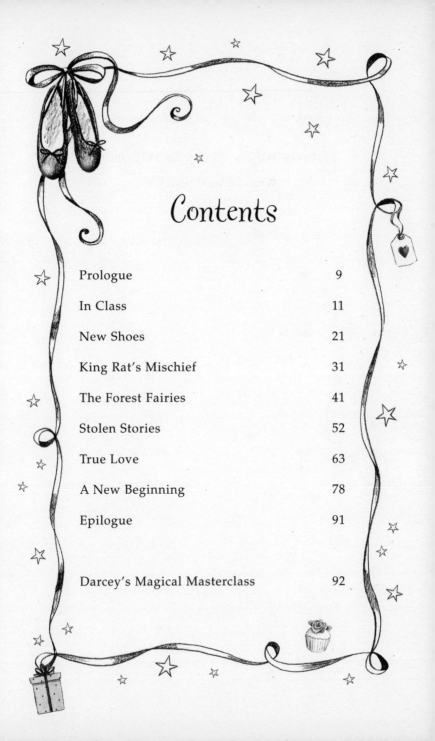

Contents

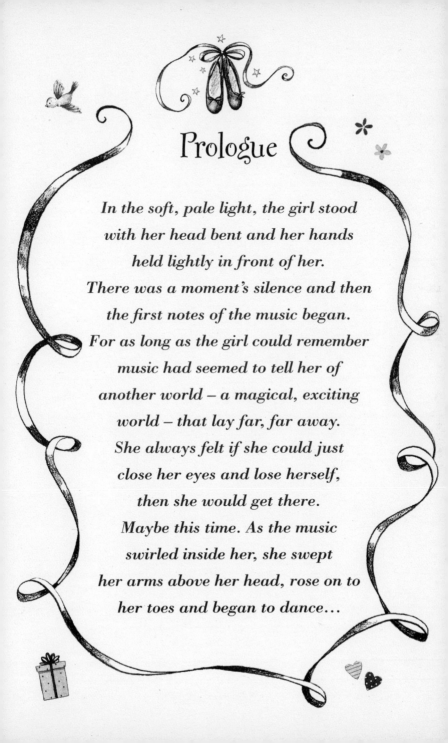

Prologue

*In the soft, pale light, the girl stood
with her head bent and her hands
held lightly in front of her.
There was a moment's silence and then
the first notes of the music began.
For as long as the girl could remember
music had seemed to tell her of
another world – a magical, exciting
world – that lay far, far away.
She always felt if she could just
close her eyes and lose herself,
then she would get there.
Maybe this time. As the music
swirled inside her, she swept
her arms above her head, rose on to
her toes and began to dance…*

In Class

Delphie sprang lightly into the air, crossing her feet over before she landed. Little jump, little jump, *pas de chat*, she thought as she sprang to the side like a cat. Stretch, bend and *pas de chat*. She landed without a single wobble, her shoulders down and her arms graceful, a smile on her face.

"Excellent, Delphie!" Madame Za-Za, her

ballet teacher, exclaimed, clapping her hands together.

Happiness rushed through Delphie as she relaxed and ran back to take her place beside the others in the class. Madame Za-Za hardly ever said "excellent".

Delphie had been having lessons at Madame Za-Za's ballet school for seven months now. Madame Za-Za had caught her watching outside the dance studio window one evening and asked her in. When she had seen Delphie dance she had offered to teach her for free – and had given her the clothes she needed and a pair of old red ballet shoes.

Delphie looked down at her shoes. They were getting very tight but she didn't want

to have new ballet shoes
because the red ones were
magic! Every so often they
would sparkle like rubies
and whisk Delphie away
to Enchantia, a magic land
where all the characters
from the different ballets
lived. Delphie had had
lots of adventures there.

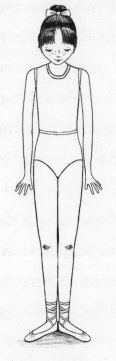

*If I have new shoes then I
won't ever get to go to
Enchantia again*, she thought. She was also
sure that the shoes helped her to dance
really well.

Trying to ignore her cramped toes, she
focused on the girl who was dancing now.

13

It was Rosa. She had only joined Madame Za-Za's ballet school a couple of months ago. She was the youngest in the class but a really good dancer and she was quickly catching up with everyone else. Delphie watched as Rosa completed the sequence. There was a wonderful energy about her dancing that Delphie really admired.

Delphie smiled and put her thumbs up as Rosa hurried back to the group. Although Rosa grinned, most of the time she kept herself to herself and Delphie didn't feel she knew much about her. *I should get to know her better*, she thought.

When the class finished they all went back to the changing rooms, chatting amongst themselves.

Delphie caught up with Rosa. "Poppy and Lola are coming back to mine on Saturday after class. Would you like to come too?"

Rosa immediatly shook her head. "I can't."

Delphie was a bit surprised at Rosa's abrupt reply. "Oh. Oh, OK, well, you'll just have to come round another time then."

15

She expected Rosa to nod but Rosa didn't.

"No. I... I really can't," she said firmly.

"What? Not ever?" Delphie frowned.

"No. Not ever. I've left my cardigan in the ballet studio!" Rosa said suddenly. "I'd better go and get it." And with that, she hurried off.

Delphie stared after her. She had the feeling Rosa had been trying to escape from talking to her. But why? She went into the changing rooms feeling very confused.

"Are you OK?" Lola asked, seeing her face.

"Mmm." Delphie sat down beside her. "I just asked Rosa if she wanted to come round on Saturday but she said no, and then she said she couldn't ever come round."

Lola and Poppy stared. "That's weird," said Poppy. "She's usually quite friendly."

Delphie spoke in a low voice, keeping one eye on the door in case Rosa came in. "I know. It's odd. I wonder why..."

But just then the door opened and Rosa came in. Delphie quickly changed the subject. "Madame Za-Za didn't say

17

anything more about us wearing pointe shoes today, did she?"

The others shook their heads.

A few days ago, Madame Za-Za had told them that she thought some of the class were ready to start dancing on their pointes. It meant wearing special ballet shoes then that had blocks in the ends so that they could stand right on their toes just like proper ballerinas. Delphie knew that it was important for people not to start using pointe shoes until their muscles were strong enough. Madame Za-Za hadn't said who in the class was almost ready but ever since she had mentioned it, Delphie, Poppy and Lola had been desperately hoping she meant them.

"My mum spoke to her when she collected me yesterday," said Lola. "Madame Za-Za said she was going to tell us more about it soon."

"Oh, I hope she says we're ready," said Poppy.

Delphie nodded. She imagined what it must be like to dance lightly on the tips of your toes and sighed longingly. She couldn't wait to have pointe shoes. *But I'll still keep my red ballet shoes*, she thought. *I'll still need normal shoes so I'll wear them too.*

But they're too small, a little voice said in the back of her mind.

19

No, they're not, Delphie thought firmly. She took them off and tried very hard to ignore the pain in her aching feet.

New Shoes

When Delphie arrived at the ballet school the next day, the first person she saw was Rosa, walking down the road from the opposite direction. Most of the girls were dropped off by their parents but Rosa always came on her own. Delphie always walked on her own too because she only lived a little way down the street.

She waited for Rosa by the gate. "Hi!"

"Oh, hi," Rosa replied.

"Where do you live?" Delphie asked curiously.

"In Hawkins Avenue," Rosa replied quickly. "It's only a few minutes away."

"It's cool being able to walk here, isn't it?" said Delphie as they went up the steps and opened the big front door. "I think my mum and dad are pleased they don't have to bring me. They're not really into ballet although they do love coming to see me in shows. Do your parents like ballet?"

"There's only me and my mum," Rosa said, shutting the door behind them. "Mum loves ballet but…" she hesitated. "Well, she can't really bring me here." She changed

the subject. "So, do you think Madame Za-Za will tell you that you can wear pointe shoes soon?"

"I hope so," replied Delphie.

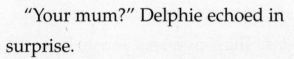

"I'd love it if she said I could," Rosa said longingly. "But I know she won't. My mum says I'm not ready yet."

"Your mum?" Delphie echoed in surprise.

"Yes, she was a…" But Rosa broke off as Madame Za-Za came out of her office.

"Ah, Delphie. Can I have a word with you?" her teacher asked.

Delphie exchanged startled looks with Rosa but Madame Za-Za was already walking back into her office. Leaving her friend to go on to the changing rooms, Delphie hurried after the teacher. Her heart pounded slightly. Maybe Madame Za-Za was about to say something about pointe shoes.

Madame Za-Za sat down in her office and patted the sofa, her bangles jingling as she did so. Delphie sat down beside her.

"Delphie, I want to talk to you. I am delighted with the progress you are making," Madame Za-Za said, smiling. "When you first came here I could see you had talent, but as well as talent you have proved you have dedication. You work very hard, you are always here to practise before class, and this shows in your dancing." Her eyes met Delphie's. "I believe it is time for you to start working on your pointes, so here you are…"

Delphie gasped in delight as Madame Za-Za handed her a cardboard box. Inside it was a new pair of pink satin pointe shoes, nestling in white tissue paper. "These are for you."

"Oh, wow!" Delphie touched the beautiful shoes.

"You are moving on." Madame Za-Za smiled. "You must have new normal shoes too. The red ballet shoes will not fit you for much longer. Maybe they are too small already?"

Delphie's stomach tightened. "No, they're fine."

Madame Za-Za looked at her searchingly. "Delphie, at some point, you will have to move on to new shoes. Just as everyone who has ever owned them before you has

done. Maybe you will even find someone to give your old shoes to."

Delphie looked down. She didn't want to stop wearing the red shoes and she certainly didn't want to give them to anyone else!

"Go and get ready for class now," Madame Za-Za told her. "You won't need your pointe shoes today. There are six of you in class who are ready to dance on pointes. I will be telling the others today and then you will all start in a new class together next week."

Delphie walked slowly out of the office. She knew she should be pleased she had pointe shoes. It was what she had been longing for but suddenly she felt as if she was on the edge of a cliff.

From now on, she'd be going to new classes and maybe she wouldn't even be with Poppy and Lola, and at some point her feet really would get too big for the red ballet shoes. *But I don't want to wear different shoes*, she thought. *I really don't want to.*

The changing rooms were empty. Rosa had already gone through to the dance studio to warm up.

Delphie got changed. It was hard to get her shoes on and her toes felt squeezed up at the end. But she couldn't give them up, she just couldn't!

Then, suddenly, her feet started to tingle. Delphie gasped. The shoes were sparkling. She was about to go to Enchantia!

She jumped up and felt herself twirling

round. Bright colours spun about her as she was lifted into the air. She forgot all about the new pointe shoes and her red shoes being too small. Excitement rushed through her. *Who was she going to meet this time?*

Would she see her friend the Sugar Plum Fairy? Or maybe Princess Aurelia? Or Cinderella? She couldn't wait to find out!

King Rat's Mischief

Delphie's feet touched firm ground and, as the swirling colours faded, she realised she was in the courtyard of the royal palace. The pearly-white turrets sparkling in the sun.

At one end of the courtyard there was a stage with forest scenery and rows of seats in front of it. It looked like a show was about to be put on, but there was no one around. Delphie wondered what was happening. She knew that the last time she had been in Enchantia, her friend Princess Aurelia had just got engaged to Prince Florimund, perhaps it was something to do with them?

Just then there was the sound of shouting from inside the palace and someone came running out. Delphie's heart leaped. It was the Sugar Plum Fairy!

Delphie was about to call out her friend's name when she saw Prince Florimund running out of the palace after her.

"Sugar, wait! I love you!" he said, throwing himself at her feet and grabbing her ballet shoes.

"Florimund!" Sugar cried crossly, pushing him away. "Stop this! I don't love you and you don't love me. You love Aurelia! Now stop being so silly and leave me alone!"

With that, she spun round with her arms

above her head, and vanished.

"She's gone!" Prince Florimund cried despairingly, staring at the empty space where Sugar had been. "My own true love has gone!" And lying on the ground he burst into tears.

Delphie stared in astonishment. *What was going on?* She was just about to go over to the prince when the palace door flew open and Aurelia came running out, her face pale. "Florimund!"

"No, Aurelia!" Prince Florimund said, scrambling to his feet. "I do not love you! I love only Sugar!" And he ran away through the palace gates.

Delphie saw Aurelia's face crumple into tears.

"Aurelia!" She raced over to her friend. "What's happening?"

The princess looked up through her tears. "Oh, Delphie! Thank goodness you're here! Please can you help me? Please!"

"I'll try. Tell me what's going on," said Delphie.

Princess Aurelia went over to a nearby bench. "Florimund doesn't love me any more," she said, taking a small mirror out of her pocket and dabbing at her tears with a lace-edged hanky. "He loves Sugar and it's all King Rat's fault!"

"King Rat," whispered Delphie, her heart

35

sinking. King Rat was horrible. He lived in a dark, smelly castle and was usually trying to cause mischief because he hated dancing. But in her last adventure in Enchantia he had actually been quite helpful and Delphie had been hoping that he might have turned over a new leaf. Now it sounded like he was up to his old tricks again! "What's he done this time?"

Aurelia sniffed. "You know Florimund and I got engaged?"

Delphie nodded.

"Well, my mother was sad at the thought of me leaving the palace to go and live with him when I got married and so to cheer her up, for her birthday I decided to organise a show of a ballet called *A Midsummer Night's*

Dream. It seemed the perfect ballet because it's all about love and my mother's birthday is on Midsummer's Day – that's today. We were going to perform it tonight. I was going to be in it with Sugar and Florimund and lots of our friends. But then it all went wrong.

"You see there's a flower in the ballet called a Love Flower. When it's squeezed on someone's eyelids they fall in love with the first person they see. King Rat snuck into the courtyard and swapped the pretend flower we were using for a real one! It was squeezed on to Florimund's eyes when we were rehearsing this morning and the first person he saw

37

was Sugar, so now he's fallen out of love with me and in love with her!"

"Oh no!" Delphie said.

"Florimund's called the wedding *and* the ballet off." Aurelia's eyes filled with fresh tears. "But the trouble is he's my true prince and I still love him! Oh, Delphie, I'm so unhappy!"

Delphie's thoughts whirled. "Why did King Rat do it?"

"Sugar said he's still upset that we

tricked him when he wanted to marry me ages ago. And of course he didn't want me to have a big wedding because that would have meant people dancing all over the land, which he hates."

Delphie thought hard. She had seen *A Midsummer Night's Dream* on TV once. She couldn't remember all of the story, but she did remember how the flower had made everyone fall in love with the wrong people. "What would happen if you squeezed the flower on the prince's eyes when he was asleep and then when he woke up he saw you? Would he fall in love with you again?"

Aurelia gasped. "Yes, I'm sure that would work!"

"Have you got one of the flowers?" Delphie asked.

Aurelia shook her head. "No. But we could get one. They grow in the woods outside the palace. They only bloom from sunrise until midday on Midsummer's Day and you have to use them before their petals droop, so we'll need to be quick." She glanced at the clock on one of the towers. "We've got about an hour before midday."

Delphie grabbed her hands. "Then let's get to the woods straight away!"

The Forest Fairies

Delphie and Aurelia hurried through the palace gates and into the forest. The trees were clustered close together and it was all very green and peaceful.

"So what does a Love Flower look like?" Delphie asked as they set off down one of the forest paths.

"It's a large pale lilac flower and it grows

41

close to the ground." Aurelia checked under some bushes. Delphie began to search the ground by the trees.

Suddenly a twig snapped behind her. She looked round quickly. But there was no one there.

As she turned to carry on searching, her eyes caught a slight movement. She continued searching but every now and then she heard a rustle in the bushes and she kept checking uneasily over her shoulder. It was as though she was being watched. She stared. Was that the end of a long thin tail sticking out from under the bushes

at the edge of the clearing? She gasped and hurried over, but by the time she got there, the tail had gone.

I must have imagined it, she thought.

"We're running out of time," Aurelia said anxiously. "I'm going to call the forest fairies, Peaseblossom, Cobweb, Moth and Mustardseed, and see if they can help. They come from *A Midsummer Night's Dream*. They're really nice. I'm sure if I summon them, they'll help."

Delphie nodded, knowing that in Enchantia it was possible to summon characters by dancing some of the steps they did in the ballets they came from.

"I'll show you the steps we have to do." Aurelia stood with her feet touching in fifth

43

position, and started to hum some music. Then she sprang upwards, crossing her feet over before doing a leap to the side and dancing forward, spinning and turning across the forest floor six times, her arms held out at shoulder height. She stopped on one leg, her body tilted forward. She held the pose before bringing her leg round and ending up in fifth position again. "Can you do that?" she asked Delphie.

"I think so," Delphie said.

Aurelia moved into place beside her. "Just imagine you're a forest sprite! Ready and…" She began to hum the music and sprang into the air.

Delphie joined in. As they finished the sequence of steps for the second time, four fairies danced out of the trees – two girls and two boys. The girl in the front was wearing a floaty white and pink ballet dress and had sweet pea flowers woven in her brown hair. She leapt lightly through the air and landed in front of Aurelia.

"Hello, Peaseblossom!" Aurelia said,
giving her a hug.

"Hello, Aurelia," the fairy said. "Why
have you summoned us?"

"We need your help," said Aurelia. "This
is Delphie."

"Pleased to meet you, Delphie. This is
Mustardseed," said Peaseblossom, pointing
to the boy in a green tunic.

"How do you do?" said Mustardseed,
sweeping into a bow.

46

"And Moth." Peaseblossom pointed to the other boy, who had large gauzy wings and a brown tunic. He bowed too.

"And this is Cobweb."

The other girl stepped forward smiling shyly. She had a pearly-grey dress and a white cap on her dark hair. "Why do you need our help?" she asked in a silvery voice.

Aurelia quickly explained. "If we don't find a Love Flower soon, Florimund will love Sugar forever."

"I know where there's a Love Flower," said Moth quickly.

"So do I," said Mustardseed.

"And I!" whispered Cobweb.

"Go, my friends!" Peaseblossom urged.

"If the flowers are still there, pick them and bring them back! Hopefully one of them at least will stay fresh until we find the prince."

The other three fairies vanished in a flash.

"Do you think they will find them before midday?" Aurelia asked anxiously.

Peaseblossom nodded reassuringly. "I'm sure they will. So how's everything at the palace?" she asked, linking arms with Aurelia and walking a little way off.

As Peaseblossom and Aurelia talked, Delphie rubbed her feet. They were really sore. She tried to move her toes but they were cramped up in her ballet shoes. Sitting down on a tree stump at the edge of the

clearing, she untied the
ribbons on her shoes.
Putting them down
behind the stump,
she wriggled her
toes, sighing with
relief.

Suddenly there
was a flash of light and the three fairies
appeared in the clearing again. They ran to
Aurelia. Delphie joined them, seeing in
delight that each fairy was carrying a lilac
flower.

"I picked mine from near a sparkling
waterfall," declared Moth.

"Mine I plucked from between the roots
of the oldest oak tree," said Mustardseed.

"And mine was growing at the edge of a field where golden corn stalks nod their stately heads," said Cobweb softly.

They handed them to Aurelia. "Oh, thank you!" she said in delight. "Now I just need to find Florimund before their petals droop and their magic fades."

"I saw the prince!" Cobweb breathed. "He was wandering through the corn field." She sighed. "He looked very sad."

"Can you take us there?" Delphie asked.

Cobweb nodded. "Of course."

"Brilliant!" Delphie ran over to the bushes to get her shoes, stopped and gasped.

"What is it?" Aurelia said.

"They've gone!" cried Delphie. "My shoes have gone!"

Stolen Shoes

Aurelia and the fairies hurried over to
Delphie. "I left them here!" she said.

"Maybe an animal took them," suggested
Moth.

"Look! There are some tracks!" Mustardseed
peered at some prints in the soft ground.
Each had four long toes and a central
splodge, and then in the middle of them

was a line that appeared to have been left by a long thin tail dragging along the ground. "Rat prints." Moth frowned. "A giant rat by the look of it."

"King Rat!" Delphie exclaimed in dismay. "It must be him! Oh no, I thought we were being followed earlier and that I saw his tail." Her eyes filled with tears. "What are we going to do? I need my shoes!"

"Don't worry," Aurelia said, hugging her. "As soon as we've put the juice on Florimund's eyelids we'll call a meeting at the palace and get everyone to help us come up with a plan. We'll get your shoes back, Delphie, I promise!" She looked at Delphie anxiously. "We can forget about

Florimund, if you like. Go to the palace straight away."

"No," Delphie shook her head, realising that would mean their plan to make the prince fall back in love with Aurelia would fail. "The Love Flowers won't last that long. Let's find the prince first and then get my shoes back."

Or try to at least, she thought, her heart sinking at the idea of horrid King Rat having her shoes.

The fairies led the way to the edge of the forest where the trees gave way to a field of golden corn with a scarecrow in the middle. Prince Florimund was wandering through

the field a little way off.
He appeared to be
pulling the kernels off
a long piece of corn
and tossing them aside.
His lips were moving
and Delphie could

see that he was saying, "She loves me, she
loves me not."

"How are we going to make him fall
asleep?" she whispered.

"We could do our Sleeping Dance,"
suggested Peaseblossom. "It makes
peaceful music start to play. Anyone who
hears it who isn't dancing will fall asleep."
She looked at Aurelia and Delphie. "You'll
both have to dance or you'll fall asleep too!"

She edged back into the shadow of the trees. "Look, these are the steps."

Delphie watched carefully. It was quite a difficult combination. Peaseblossom repeated it twice.

"It looks hard," Delphie said.

"Don't worry," said Aurelia. "You'll be able to do it."

"I wish I had my shoes," said Delphie unhappily. "They help me to dance."

"No, they don't," Aurelia told her. "You just think that but it's your heart and your feet that do the dancing, not your shoes, I promise." She squeezed Delphie's hands. "You can do this. I know you can!"

Aurelia and Delphie joined the fairies. Peaseblossom nodded and they all started to dance. Delphie tried to remember the slow, graceful steps. She turned about, one arm above her head and the other sweeping round, then she stepped forward into an *arabesque* with her left leg held out behind her. She ran forward three steps and then spun.

Soft music flooded through the air. "The magic's working!" called Peaseblossom.

Delphie felt her heart lift. With the music playing, the steps of the dance came even more easily. The dreamy notes floated out across the cornfield. The prince looked round in surprise. He yawned and sat down. A few seconds later he was sound asleep.

"We've done it!" cried Delphie.

Aurelia ran to the prince and squeezed the flower above his eyes. Two drops fell from the pale petals and landed on his eyelids. The fairies stopped dancing and the music faded away.

"Quick, hide, everyone!" Delphie said. "Aurelia, you wake up the prince!"

Delphie and the fairies peeped out from behind trees as Aurelia sat next to the prince. She stroked his brown hair. Delphie saw him stretch and open his eyes.

Oh, please let it have worked, Delphie thought anxiously.

A smile spread across Florimund's face. "Aurelia."

"Florimund!" whispered Aurelia.

"I have had the strangest dream!" cried the prince, sitting up. "Oh, Aurelia. I dreamed I was in love with Sugar."

"It wasn't a dream, Florimund," Aurelia said.

"It wasn't?"

Aurelia shook her head and, as Delphie and the fairies came out from behind the trees, the princess told Florimund what had happened to him and about Delphie's shoes going missing too.

"Oh, Aurelia, I am so sorry," he said, looking horrified. "I love you. You are my true princess. It must have been the

enchantment that made me think differently. Please will you marry me after all?"

"Of course I will!" smiled Aurelia.

Florimund jumped up and swung her round. "And we'll put on the ballet like we planned for your mother's birthday!" He pulled out his sword. "But first we have to get back Delphie's shoes."

"Oh, Florimund," cried Aurelia in delight. "You're so brave!"

A loud snoring noise suddenly made them all jump. "What's that?" Delphie said.

"It's coming from over there!" replied Mustardseed, pointing to the edge of the field.

They all hurried over. Lying in the corn was a fat figure with black greasy fur, a belt with a sword, a red cloak and a golden crown. His eyes were shut and loud snores were issuing from his long snout, making his curly whiskers quiver and wobble.

Delphie gasped. "It's King Rat!"

True Love

"King Rat must have been passing through the field trying to escape with your ballet shoes and then heard the music and fallen asleep," whispered Peaseblossom.

"Ssh, don't wake him!" said Cobweb anxiously.

"Look!" hissed Aurelia. "Delphie's ballet shoes are sticking out of his bag!"

A brown sack was lying beside King Rat and the two red ballet shoes could be seen at the top.

"I'll get them!" Prince Florimund crept forward and took out the shoes. He hurried back to the others and handed them to Delphie.

Delphie smiled in delight. "Oh, thank you!" she said, quickly slipping them on.

"Now we can get back to the palace!" declared Florimund.

"First, I think we should play a trick on King Rat," Peaseblossom said mischievously. She whispered in the other fairies' ears. They giggled and then raced off towards the raggedy scarecrow in the middle of the field. It was wearing a dress and had a head made out of an old stuffed sack with large eyes and a mouth painted on. As they set the scarecrow down beside King Rat, Peaseblossom squeezed the juice from the flowers on to his eyelids and prodded him with her finger.

King Rat grumbled in his sleep. Peaseblossom dashed away. King Rat sat up scratching his greasy

head and then suddenly saw the
scarecrow. He drew in a deep breath.
"What beautiful lady is this before me?"
he said in astonishment.

Delphie put her hand over her mouth to
stop herself giggling. The fairies had made
King Rat fall in love with a scarecrow!

King Rat scrambled to his feet. "You, madam, are divine!" He swept into a low bow. "My name is King Rat. Yes, I know," he said raising up a hand as if to stop the scarecrow from speaking. "You are struck dumb by my charm. I often have that effect on people. But you," he walked around her admiringly, "are a match truly worthy of me. Your eyes! Your smile! Your beautiful straw-like hair! I have never seen such beauty in all my life! Will you do me the honour of being my wife?"

Cobweb giggled. "Doesn't King Rat look silly?"

"Serves him right for taking Delphie's shoes," said Peaseblossom. "And for causing all this trouble in the first place."

Aurelia grinned. "Come on, let's go back to the palace now."

"But we can't just leave King Rat in love with a scarecrow!" protested Delphie. It was funny but also slightly mean. "What will happen when the scarecrow falls apart?"

"Hmm," said Aurelia as King Rat kissed the scarecrow's floppy hand. "I suppose you're right."

"But what are we going to do?" said Moth. "There's no cure from the Love Flower's enchantment apart from making him fall in love with someone else."

Delphie thought for a moment and then

had an idea. "Aurelia, have you got your little pocket mirror?"

Aurelia nodded.

Delphie grinned. "Then I think I might have a plan!"

Ten minutes later, King Rat was snoring loudly, sent to sleep once more by the Sleeping Dance. The scarecrow had been removed and now Aurelia's mirror was open beside him. Delphie clapped her hands loudly and King Rat woke with a start. As he did so, his eyes fell on the mirror.

He gave a snort of delight as he saw his own reflection. "Well, look at me. I'm even

69

more gorgeous than normal today!" he
said, acting impressed. He preened his
whiskers. "What a fine figure of rathood I
am!" He tickled his nose in the mirror and
sighed happily. "I think I'm going to just
look at myself all day long!"

Aurelia chuckled. "That was a brilliant
idea, Delphie! Now you'd hardly know
King Rat was enchanted at all!"

"Our job is done here," said
Peaseblossom. "You should get back to the

palace and tell everyone the ballet show is on after all!"

"There's going to be so much to do to get it organised in time," Aurelia said. "Will you come and see it tonight?"

"We'd love to!" said Moth.

"See you later!" called Aurelia and then she, Delphie and the prince ran back to the palace.

When they arrived back and said the ballet show was on again, everyone began to rush around getting ready. Delphie found herself caught up in the whirl of preparation, helping to sew the final bits of costumes while all around her the dancers rehearsed.

It was great fun and she didn't mind at all that she wasn't dancing in the show. She just couldn't wait to watch it!

At last it was time to sit down. Delphie had the honour of sitting with King Tristan and Queen Isabella.

The show was great, the prince, Aurelia, Sugar and one of the prince's friends, Prince Siegfried, were playing two couples who were in love. There was also a fairy king and queen and their fairy attendants, and a group of funny men who were supposed to be practising for a play. Delphie loved it. And so did the Queen!

She clapped and clapped at the end and the cast had to bow ten times. "Oh, I'm so glad Aurelia is marrying Prince Florimund,"

Delphie heard the Queen say to the King.
"That was the most wonderful birthday
treat ever!"

Afterwards there was a big party to
celebrate. Sugar came to find Delphie.
"Thank you so much for helping sort
everything out," she said as they walked a
bit away from the throng. I'm very glad
Florimund isn't in love with me any more
and it was brilliant to be able to perform
the ballet after all!"

"It's been a really fun adventure," said
Delphie. "I'm glad it's ended happily. Even
King Rat is pleased to be in love with
himself!"

"So, it's happily ever after for everyone!"
smiled Sugar.

"Well, not quite," Delphie said quietly, bending her aching toes in her tight shoes.

Sugar looked at her curiously. "What do you mean?"

Delphie bit her lip and her fears came rushing out. "Oh, Sugar. My magic ballet shoes are getting too small. I know now that I can dance just as well without them, but if I can't fit them on my feet, I can't come here and visit you."

Sugar took her hand. "But you won't be giving up Enchantia forever. It is not only the shoes that can bring you here."

"Really?" said Delphie hopefully.

"Really," Sugar insisted. "Enchantia is always going to be here waiting for you, Delphie. Dance with your heart and you *will* return."

The band struck up a polka. Sugar grabbed Delphie's hands. "Come on!"

They were swept away in the lively dance. Delphie's head spun as she and Sugar swung each other round. She laughed out loud in delight and then, as the dance ended, her shoes began to sparkle and glow.

"I'm going home!" Delphie gasped.

Sugar hugged her. "See you soon, I hope! Bye, Delphie!"

A myriad of colours suddenly surrounded

Delphie. She whizzed round and round until her feet landed on solid ground. She blinked as she found herself back in the quiet changing rooms. No time had passed at all.

Delphie looked down at her shoes and touched them. She knew now she could dance without her magic shoes and that she would be able to get to Enchantia without them, but she still didn't feel ready to give them up.

Madame Za-Za's words rang in her head: *You will know when the time is right,* she had said.

But when will that be? Delphie thought. *When?*

A New Beginning

Delphie and Rosa were the last to leave after class that day. As they walked out of the ballet school, Rosa called goodbye and headed off to the right. Delphie turned to the left and then stopped. She realised she hadn't said anything to Rosa about the pointe shoes. At the end of class, Madame Za-Za had said that Delphie, Poppy, Lola,

Sukie, Anna and Megan were the six girls who would be moving into a new class. Rosa hadn't been selected. *She must be really disappointed*, Delphie thought. *I would have been.*

She hesitated. Maybe she should go and talk to her? She turned, Rosa was already crossing the road and heading down Hawkins Avenue. Delphie made up her mind and ran back. She crossed the road just as Rosa went into a bungalow with a green door halfway down the street.

Delphie jogged down the pavement. She'd just check Rosa wasn't too upset.

She reached the green front door and knocked. Rosa opened it. She looked shocked and, if anything, a bit put out.

"Delphie! What… what are you doing here?"

"I came to see you. I was worried you might be upset about not getting to dance on your pointes and coming to the next

class with us," Delphie said.

"Well, I'm just fine," Rosa said. "I'd expected it. Look, Delphie, thanks for coming but I have to go!"

As Rosa started to shut the door on Delphie, a voice called out, "Rosa! Who's there?"

"It's OK, Mum. It's just a friend," Rosa said quickly.

80

A woman came into the hall in a wheelchair. She was very beautiful with long blonde hair tied back in a low bun, huge blue eyes and a very friendly face. "Hello," she said to Delphie.

Delphie looked across at Rosa, who now was positively glaring at her. Why was she looking so cross?

"Hello," Delphie said to Rosa's mum, politely holding out her hand. "I'm Delphie Durand."

Rosa's mum smiled. "I'm Nicolette Maitland. I'm very pleased to meet you, Delphie. I'd love to come and watch Rosa do ballet and meet all her new friends but it's quite hard for me to get into the ballet school because of those steps. Did Rosa tell you I used to be a ballerina myself?"

"No," said Delphie in astonishment. She couldn't help herself from looking at Mrs Maitland's wheelchair.

Mrs Maitland followed her gaze. "I had a car accident," she explained. "So I had to retire from ballet." She saw Delphie's face. "It was sad but then afterwards I had Rosa. Now I wouldn't want it to be any different." She looked at a photo on the wall of a ballerina caught gracefully in mid-jump. "That was me, back when I was dancing."

Delphie looked from the picture to Mrs Maitland in awe. "Wow! I've never met a real ballerina before. Well, apart from Madame Za-Za!"

Mrs Maitland smiled. "Would you like to stay for tea? We could give your parents a ring. I'm always telling Rosa she should bring more friends home."

"I'd love to!" Delphie said, eager to talk to Mrs Maitland some more.

After phoning to check it was OK, Delphie went to Rosa's bedroom. "Why didn't you tell me about your mum?" she said as soon as the door was shut.

"What? That she's in a wheelchair?" said Rosa in a tight voice.

"No!" That thought hadn't even crossed Delphie's mind. "Why didn't you say that she used to be a ballerina! That's so cool and…" She broke off, realising what Rosa had just said. "Hang on, did you think your mum being in a wheelchair would worry me or something?"

Rosa bit her lip and nodded. "Before we moved I had friends from school come round a few times and well… they weren't very nice about Mum. I got teased about her wheelchair afterwards."

"But that's horrible!" Delphie exclaimed, suddenly understanding why Rosa had seemed so unwelcoming at the door.

Rosa swallowed. "When we moved I didn't want it all to happen again so I thought I just wouldn't have anyone back for tea or go to anyone's house."

"Well, I think you're really lucky to have a mum who was a ballerina, and who's so lovely," Delphie declared. "And I know Poppy and Lola would feel just the same."

Rosa breathed out. "You mean that?"

"Of course I do!" smiled Delphie. She looked around at the photos on Rosa's walls. Many of them were of her mum. "What part was she dancing here… and here…?"

Delphie listened, entranced, while Rosa proudly told her about her mum's past and then, while they had tea, Mrs Maitland told Delphie all about her training at the Royal Ballet School and how her dearest wish was that Rosa would one day go there too. Afterwards they went back to Rosa's room to get Delphie's things.

"You must be so pleased that you're getting to wear pointe shoes," Rosa said, looking at the cardboard box.

Delphie nodded. "I just wish Madame

Za-Za had said you could wear them too."

"It's OK. I didn't think she would," Rosa said. "But I'm going to practise lots and it won't be long before I am ready. Until then, I'll just have to make do with normal shoes."

As Delphie looked at the younger girl she suddenly knew what she had to do. "Rosa, would you like my old red ballet shoes?"

Rosa stared. "But didn't Madame Za-Za give them to you?"

"She did, but my feet are getting too big for them now and I think she'll be pleased I'm giving them to you." Delphie pulled the shoes out of her bag and held them out. "Here."

Rosa took them wonderingly. "Oh, wow. Thank you, Delphie!"

Delphie looked at the shoes, sitting in Rosa's hands, their red leather gleaming. "They're very special shoes," she said softly. "But I'm sure you'll find that out." She grinned. "Just watch out for King Rat though."

Rosa looked at her in astonishment. "What?"

"You'll see!"

Delphie left Rosa's house feeling light and happy. She was moving forward and she knew that the right time had come to pass the red shoes on.

I hope I do get to go to Enchantia again though, she thought.

Sugar's words suddenly seemed to echo in her head: *Dance with your heart and you will return.*

Delphie smiled and hugging her new pointe shoes to her chest, she ran down the street.

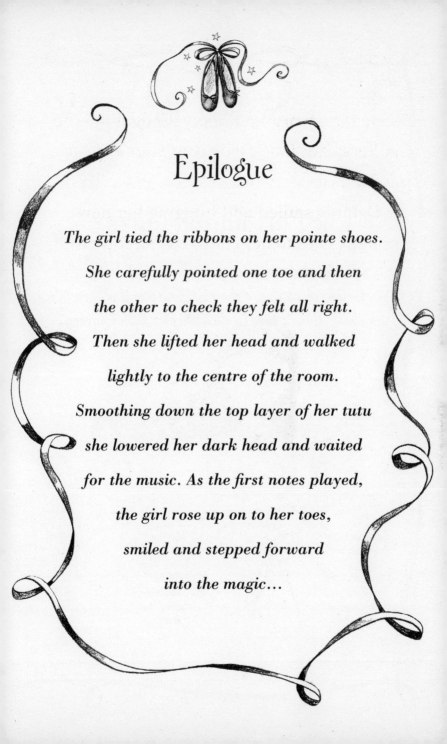

Epilogue

The girl tied the ribbons on her pointe shoes.
She carefully pointed one toe and then
the other to check they felt all right.
Then she lifted her head and walked
lightly to the centre of the room.
Smoothing down the top layer of her tutu
she lowered her dark head and waited
for the music. As the first notes played,
the girl rose up on to her toes,
smiled and stepped forward
into the magic...

Darcey's Magical Masterclass

The Curtain-call Curtsy

Ballet dancers curtsy at the end of every performance to thank their audience and others in the show. Here's how to do a perfect ballet curtsy...

1.
Start in first position and then point your left foot out the side, opening up your arms.

2.
Slide your left foot behind your right foot without letting it leave the floor.

3.
Gently bend
both your
knees and
lower into
your curtsy.

4.
Straighten up,
bringing your
left leg back to
rest in the
centre again
and lower
your arms.

Magic Ballerina™

Have you read all of Delphie's magical adventures?

Magic Ballerina — *Delphie and the Magic Ballet Shoes* — Darcey Bussell

Magic Ballerina — *Delphie and the Magic Spell* — Darcey Bussell

Magic Ballerina — *Delphie and the Masked Ball* — Darcey Bussell

Magic Ballerina — *Delphie and the Glass Slippers* — Darcey Bussell

Magic Ballerina — *Delphie and the Fairy Godmother* — Darcey Bussell

Magic Ballerina — *Delphie and the Birthday Show* — Darcey Bussell

Join Rosa in the next series of

Magic Ballerina

as she enters the wonderful

world of Enchantia!

Make sure you have your

dancing shoes ready…

www.magicballerina.com

Darcey Bussell

Buy more great Magic Ballerina books direct from HarperCollins at **10%** off recommended retail price.
FREE postage and packing in the UK.

Delphie and the Magic Ballet Shoes	ISBN 978 0 00 728607 2
Delphie and the Magic Spell	ISBN 978 0 00 728608 9
Delphie and the Masked Ball	ISBN 978 0 00 728610 2
Delphie and the Glass Slippers	ISBN 978 0 00 728617 1
Delphie and the Fairy Godmother	ISBN 978 0 00 728611 9
Delphie and the Birthday Show	ISBN 978 0 00 728612 6

All priced at £3.99

To purchase by Visa/Mastercard/Switch simply call
08707871724 or fax on **08707871725**

To pay by cheque, send a copy of this form with a cheque made payable to
'HarperCollins Publishers' to: Mail Order Dept. (Ref: BOB4),
HarperCollins Publishers, Westerhill Road, Bishopbriggs, G64 2QT,
making sure to include your full name, postal address and phone number.

From time to time HarperCollins may wish to use your personal data
to send you details of other HarperCollins publications and offers.
If you wish to receive information on other HarperCollins publications
and offers please tick this box ☐

Do not send cash or currency. Prices correct at time of press.
Prices and availability are subject to change without notice.
Delivery overseas and to Ireland incurs a £2 per book postage and packing charge.